Mommy Time

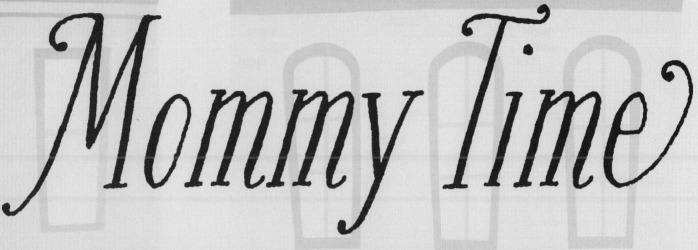

Mommy Time

MONIQUE JAMES-DUNCAN
ILLUSTRATED BY EBONY GLENN

CANDLEWICK PRESS

Wake up! Sun's up. It's morning time,
and we just love our Mommy time.

She drags us out of bed time,
then it's comb our bushy hair time

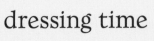 

 breakfast time.

Pack up lunch, a tasty munch,
and off sister goes to school time.

Come in. Join in.
It's sing-along time,
and I just love my Mommy time.

She clasps my hands in hers time,
then conga drums, *shack-shack* time . . .

dancing time

gleeful time.

Blocks in a row. We have to go?
Please . . . let's stay for longer time?

Can't stop, won't stop. It's *our* time,
and I just love my Mommy time.
She wheels me through the market time . . .

then it's swings for fun at the playground time
laughing time
friendship time.
Chitchat with you! *Ga-ga goo-goo!*

It's pick sister up from school time,
then off to violin time . . .

or library time

or playdate time.

Or dentist too? So much to do!
Be sure we're right on time, time.

Calm stroll, fun stroll. It's go-home time,
and sister just loves her Mommy time.
Mommy asks about her day time.
Her friends? Her dreams? They talk time.

Kickball time.

Leaves fall time.

Love in her eyes,
care in her smiles.
Tender, precious
moments time.

Slow down, wind down. It's evening time,
and we just love our Mommy time.
She helps with any homework time,
then it's eat green beans and chicken stew time.

Then it's bath time,

story time.

Feel her tickles, kiss her dimples.

Yawn . . . we love our Mommy time.

For my mommy and daddy, Wilma and Edison.
And for my husband, Charles, and children, Zo and Samory.
MJ-D

For Luna
EG

First edition 2023

Library of Congress Catalog Card Number 2022907013
ISBN 978-1-5362-1226-6

22 23 24 25 26 27 CCP 10 9 8 7 6 5 4 3 2 1

Printed in Shenzhen, Guangdong, China

This book was typeset in Veronan.
The illustrations were created digitally.

Candlewick Press
99 Dover Street
Somerville, Massachusetts 02144

www.candlewick.com